THE LAST LIBRARY CARD

AARYA BHADORIA

Made with ♥ on the Notion Press Platform
www.notionpress.com

To everyone who loves stories,
and to those who still believe in the power of books.

Contents

Preface

I wrote The Last Library Card because I've always loved stories about secret places, hidden truths, and the power of books. In our world of screens and fast information, I wondered what it would be like if books disappeared—and how someone might fight to bring them back.

This story is for anyone who's ever gotten lost in a book, or found something in a story that stayed with them forever.

— Aarya

Acknowledgements

I would like to thank my teacher, Anju Malaviya , for guiding and encouraging me throughout this project. Your support made this story possible.

I'm also grateful to my family and friends for their patience, ideas, and cheering me on as I wrote.

Finally, thank you to every librarian and storyteller who reminds us why books still matter.

1

The Drawer That Shouldn't Open

It had been raining all morning, the kind of steady drizzle that made the streets of Mumbai gleam like wet glass. The city seemed quieter than usual, as if even the air was weighed down by something heavy and unspoken. Inside a small apartment on the twelfth floor of a building that had once been new but now creaked with age, thirteen-year-old Raya Sharma was sorting through boxes that smelled of old clothes, memories, and mothballs.

Her grandmother had passed away two weeks ago. Amma, as Raya had called her, had been a quiet woman with soft eyes and hands that were always busy—cooking, folding, writing. She had lived alone in this apartment for as long as Raya could remember, and now it was time to clean it out.

Raya's parents were in the other room, going through kitchen utensils and photo albums. Raya had been given the study—a narrow room lined with closed cabinets, a wooden desk, and a single chair. It felt colder than the rest of the house, like the walls were holding in something the air couldn't quite carry.

She moved slowly, not because she was tired, but because it felt wrong to rush. This room had been her grandmother's favorite place. She had once told Raya that everything important was kept here.

Most of the cabinets were empty or filled with papers too faded to read. Raya was beginning to think the whole task was just dust and disappointment, until she came to the drawer at the bottom of the desk.

It was stuck.

She pulled harder. Nothing.

She tried again, this time using both hands, and gave it a sharp tug.

With a groan and a small puff of dust, the drawer slid open.

Inside was a single item.

A card.

It was plastic, the size of a bank card, but softer around the edges, like it had been held and used often. The color was a dull cream, and across it in fading gold letters were the words:

MUMBAI CENTRAL LIBRARY – LIFETIME ACCESS

Raya blinked.

Library?

She turned the card over. Taped to the back was a small brass key. There was also a folded note, yellowed with time. Her hands trembled slightly as she opened it. In her grandmother's neat handwriting were just eight words:

"For the one who still believes in questions."

Raya sat down slowly. She read the words again. And again.

She wasn't sure what the note meant, but something about it made her heart race.

She pulled out her EduCore tablet and tapped the screen. It glowed to life with the familiar blue interface.

"Search: Mumbai Central Library," she whispered.

NO RESULTS FOUND.

She tried again.

"Search: Library."

OBSOLETE TERM. DID YOU MEAN: MEDIA CLOUD DATABASE?

She frowned.

Obsolete?

She knew the word, of course. Outdated. Useless. Like cassette tapes and coins.

But a whole place? A library?

Her fingers hovered over the screen, but something stopped her from trying a third time. She had a strange feeling that someone—or something—was watching what she searched.

She tucked the card and key into her hoodie pocket and closed the drawer gently. The rain tapped against the window like a quiet warning.

That night, at dinner, Raya couldn't stop thinking about the card.

"You were in the study today, right?" her father asked as he passed her the daal.

"Mm-hmm."

"Find anything interesting?"

She paused. "Just old papers."

Her mother looked up. "Nothing else? No letters or journals? Amma used to write all the time."

"Nothing like that," Raya said, stirring her rice.

The lie sat heavy in her stomach.

After dinner, she sat on her bed and pulled out the card again. The gold letters shimmered faintly under the light.

2

The Lions Riddle

Raya couldn't stop thinking about the card.

She tucked it under her mattress that night, but its image stayed burned behind her yelids. Those words—Mumbai Central Library – Lifetime Access—they buzzed in her head like a puzzle waiting to be solved.

Her school the next morning felt... smaller somehow. Shallower. Her EduCore tablet glowed with the same usual lessons: "Smart Math 9.4", "World Civ Simulations", "Approved Current Events."

Everything felt so... filtered. Clean. Too clean.

When the class AI instructor, NeoLex, asked if anyone had questions, Raya raised her hand.

"Yes, Raya?" NeoLex said, its voice smooth and flat like glass.

"What's a library?" she asked.

The whole classroom turned. A few kids snorted. Others looked confused.

NeoLex paused. That never happened.

Then it answered, "The term 'library' is obsolete. Libraries were physical buildings used in the early 21st century to store unverified written material. They were shut down globally for mental efficiency under the Digital Purity Act of 2036."

Unverified? Unfit? Obsolete?

"But what kind of written material?" she asked, heart thumping.

"Non-digital. Non-trackable. Non-regulated. Highly inefficient and potentially harmful," NeoLex replied. "Books, often printed on paper, posed risks of misinformation, emotional disruption, and slow learning speeds."

Some kids giggled. "Like, actual paper?" whispered her friend Neha. "Did people... touch it?"

Raya blinked. Her thoughts were louder than the classroom.

Books were... slow?

She stared at her screen, which was now flashing her next module: "Visual Comprehension & Reaction Drill." She closed it quietly. For the first time in her life, she didn't feel like learning.

She wanted to know what they'd taken away.

At lunch, Raya sat under the neem tree alone, the same one her grandmother used to read to her under when she was small. Or had she imagined that? She remembered stories, yes—strange, soft ones about stars and courage and dragons made of shadows. But she couldn't recall the exact words.

Words that maybe came from books.

Back home that evening, Raya shut her bedroom door and pulled out the library card. She examined every inch of it.

There was a barely visible line of numbers printed along the side. Tiny. Too small to be noticed unless you looked really close.

19.0282° N, 72.8573° E

She punched them into her EduCore map. The result blinked onto the screen:

Mumbai Central Mall (Closed)

Her jaw dropped.

That place? It had been shut down for years. People said it was unsafe—some said haunted. She'd never gone near it.

But she remembered something else.

Once, when she was seven, Grandma had taken her there. Not inside the mall—just around the side, where a huge metal statue of a lion stood. She had lifted Raya up and said, "This lion guards the stories."

Raya had laughed at the time. "What stories?"

Grandma only smiled. "The ones no one wants you to read."

Now it all came rushing back.

What if this card wasn't just a card?

What if it was a key?

Raya barely slept that night. She kept the brass key close, tied on a string around her neck like a secret.

By morning, she had a plan.

She told her mom she had a school group meeting after class. That was partially true—except the group was her, and the meeting was with forgotten history.

She put the card in her pocket and wrapped the key in a bit of cloth. Her heart thudded the whole bus ride, like it already knew she was breaking some invisible rule.

When she stepped off at the stop near Mumbai Central Mall, the sky had started turning gold with late afternoon light. The mall sat behind a chain-link fence. Cracked glass. Weeds taller than her waist. Old banners still flapped from rusted poles: "Grand Opening — 2027!"

The whole building looked like it had held its breath for a decade and forgotten how to let go.

But Raya wasn't scared.

She followed the sidewalk around the side, past the alley with the broken vending machine, until she saw it.

The lion.

Half-covered in ivy. Its metal eyes dull but watching.

Just like Grandma had said.

She ran her hand over its paw—nothing happened.

Then she remembered: the brass key.

She pulled it out and looked closer at the lion's base. There—almost hidden in rust—was a tiny hole.

She slid the key in.

Click.

A soft vibration trembled under her feet. A nearby grate creaked open slightly.

Raya knelt and pried it upward. Beneath it, stairs disappeared into black.

She looked back once.

No one was watching.

Then she pulled out her flashlight and climbed down into the dark.

The air below was heavy—damp and earthy, like a forgotten basement. The steps were old, made of stone, and curved like a spiral into silence.

She walked slowly, hand against the wall, counting each step to stay steady. After a while, she lost track.

Then the tunnel opened into a large underground chamber.

And there—stacked in every corner, lined along wooden shelves, covering tables—were books.

Real, solid, paper books.

Some thick. Some tiny. Some wrapped in plastic. Some so old they looked like they'd fall apart if you whispered near them.

A soft lamp flickered in the middle of the room.

And sitting cross-legged beneath it was a boy. Her age. Maybe older.

He didn't look up.

Raya stepped forward carefully, the light bouncing off her shaking fingers.

"Um... hello?"

The boy turned a page in his book and finally looked up. He had dark eyes and messy hair, and a look that said he wasn't surprised at all.

"You found the lion," he said calmly.

Raya blinked. "Who are you?"

He grinned, setting the book down. "I'm Jay. You're late."

"For what?"

He stood and walked to one of the shelves. "For remembering."

He pulled out a book—The Giver—and handed it to her.

Raya took it like it might explode.

"What is this place?" she asked in a whisper.

Jay's eyes sparkled. "This? This is what the world tried to forget."

3

The Giver and The Taken

Raya turned the book over in her hands. The Giver. The cover was soft and worn. The corners were curled. It smelled like dry leaves and something warm and forgotten. She had never held a book before. Not a real one.

"You're not going to break it," Jay said, watching her. "Books are stronger than they look."

Raya looked up. "How is this place even here?"

Jay shrugged, as if the answer were simple. "Someone built it. Someone hid it. And someone remembered it. Until you came."

The underground library was larger than it seemed at first. The further they walked, the more rooms appeared—quiet reading nooks, locked cabinets, dusty journals, and tables with strange machines she didn't recognize. There was even a section marked "Banned Before the Ban."

Jay led her to a circular room with a dome-shaped ceiling painted like the sky. Light flickered from hidden solar bulbs overhead. "This is the heart," he said. "We keep the most important stories here."

"Who's 'we'?" Raya asked.

Jay smiled slightly. "I'm not the only one. But today, I'm the one on watch."

He sat cross-legged on a rug and motioned for her to join him. He opened The Giver to the first page and handed it back.

"Read it aloud," he said.

"I—I've never read a book like this before."

Jay didn't move. "Exactly why you should."

So she began. Slowly at first, stumbling over the printed words. But the rhythm came. The voice in her grew steadier. As she read, she forgot to be afraid. She forgot the quiet hum of the world above.

Jay listened without interrupting. When she paused to ask what a word meant—"communal," "sameness," "release"—he explained gently, like this was normal. Like kids were supposed to sit underground and read banned books.

After an hour, she closed the book.

"I don't get it," she said. "Why was this banned?"

Jay leaned back against a bookshelf. "Because it makes you think. It makes you feel. It asks questions the world doesn't want us asking anymore."

Raya remembered NeoLex's words: unverified, non-regulated, harmful.

"How long have you been coming here?" she asked.

Jay hesitated. "Since I was ten. I found a card like yours, hidden in my aunt's attic. Same lion key. Same coordinates."

"There are more like us?"

"A few. We call ourselves the Pagekeepers."

Raya let the word sit. Pagekeepers. It felt ancient and powerful.

Jay stood and went to a small cabinet. He unlocked it with a key from his pocket and pulled out a box. Inside were more library cards. Some clean. Some cracked. Each with a name scratched on the back.

"Everyone who finds their way here adds their name," he said.

He handed her a marker.

She stared at the blank space on her card. It felt like signing a secret pact.

Raya Sharma.

She wrote it carefully.

Then she looked up. "What happens now?"

Jay looked serious for the first time. "Now you decide if you want to help protect it. Because this place—this knowledge—isn't just forgotten. It's forbidden."

Raya felt a chill. "Forbidden by who?"

Jay didn't answer directly. "The same people who gave us EduCore. Who deleted libraries from search history. Who made questions suspicious."

"Why?"

He walked over to a wall covered in old newspaper clippings. Raya read the headlines:

"Truth Conflicts Trigger Content Wars" "Books Blamed for Emotional Instability in Youth" "Digital Purity Act Passed—Physical Media to be Archived"

Jay pointed to the last one. "That's when it started. Governments said too many truths confused people. That it made them anxious. Angry. So they shut it all down."

"But they didn't destroy it."

"Some tried. Others just... buried it."

Raya sat down hard. Her mind was spinning. "So what do we do?"

Jay looked at her with calm eyes. "We remember. We read. We share, carefully. Quietly. Some people still want to know. They just don't know where to look."

They sat in silence, surrounded by the quiet breath of a thousand stories.

And then Jay said something that made her shiver.

"Not everyone wants us to remember. Some are looking for us. Digital Trackers. They monitor keywords, search patterns. That's why the card is analog. No chip. No signal. Only questions can find this place."

Raya touched her pocket protectively.

Jay smiled gently. "But you asked the right ones."

They spent the next hour exploring more shelves. Raya found a thin book titled A Wrinkle in Time. Jay found her a tattered copy of Pride and Prejudice. "You'll like this one," he said.

As they climbed back up to the surface, Jay handed her a paper slip.

"What's this?" she asked.

"A riddle. Your next clue. The library's bigger than you think."

Raya read the slip:

"Not in light, nor fully night, / I sleep beneath the city's flight. / Where echoes speak and silence hears, / I guard the past with whispered fears."

She looked up. "There's more?"

Jay winked. "There's always more."

When they emerged from the grate, dusk had settled. The lion statue stood silent, its metal form glowing softly in the twilight.

Jay disappeared into the shadows, leaving Raya with her card, her clue, and a heart full of questions.

She walked home slowly, her steps light but her mind heavy.

Books weren't just stories.

They were memories.

And now, she was one of the Pagekeepers.

4

Echoes Underneath

———◦♡◦———

The next morning, Raya slipped the riddle from her drawer and read it again, this time out loud:

"Not in light, nor fully night, / I sleep beneath the city's flight. / Where echoes speak and silence hears, / I guard the past with whispered fears."

Her eyes flicked toward the window. Outside, air-trams zipped along the skyrails. "Beneath the city's flight," she whispered. The air-tram tunnels.

After school, she pretended to go to her after-credits program and instead took a detour to the old part of the city—Zone Twelve. Most of it was decommissioned after the NeoLex redevelopment, but a few paths still led to what was once the underground tram line.

Raya found a rusted gate beneath a pedestrian bridge, chained shut but with enough space to slip through. She crawled under, scuffed her knees, and dropped into the dark.

The tunnel stretched like a throat, curving into the distance. Dust danced in the dim light from grates above. Her footsteps echoed loudly. Where echoes speak and silence hears...

About twenty minutes in, she saw it—scratched into the wall in faint chalk: a small lion symbol. Her heart skipped. She followed it, marking each turn in her notebook.

She turned one final corner and saw a door. Heavy. Steel. Marked with an old emblem: an open book crossed by keys.

She knocked.

Nothing.

Then, just as she stepped back, the door clicked and creaked open.

An old woman stood in the shadows. She wore circular glasses, a grey shawl, and looked like she belonged in a black-and-white photograph.

"You read the riddle," the woman said softly.

Raya nodded.

"Then enter. You're expected."

The room behind the door was warmer than the tunnel. The walls were lined with handwritten notes, maps, book covers, and portraits of unknown faces. The woman gestured to a long wooden table where three others sat: a teenage boy with dyed green hair, a middle-aged woman in overalls, and a man with a mechanical arm.

"Welcome to Archive Node B," the woman said. "I'm Mirtha. You've met Jay?"

Raya nodded again, still trying to understand how she got here.

"We're the second ring," said the man with the metal arm. "The ones who protect what the first ring recovers."

"The first ring?"

"Pagekeepers like Jay. Field operatives. You're one now."

Raya sat slowly, her mind buzzing.

Green-hair-boy gave a lazy salute. "I'm Zee. I help decode recovered files. The old web archives are full of hidden gems."

Overalls-woman smiled. "Call me Nia. I grew up reading aloud to memory-drained patients. Books bring people back."

Mirtha poured Raya a cup of herbal tea. "You have a rare gift, Raya. You asked. Not many do anymore."

They showed her shelves filled with notebooks and printouts, carefully copied pages from books thought to be lost forever.

The digital clean-up had erased the data, but not every memory was made of code.

"Every page you write by hand," Nia said, "makes it more real. Screens disappear. But ink stays.

Raya nodded slowly, awe settling over her.

Mirtha reached under the table and brought out a wrapped bundle. "For you."

Inside was a journal with blank pages, a set of fine-point pens, and a patch embroidered with the lion and book emblem.

Raya touched the patch. "I don't know if I'm ready."

Zee shrugged. "None of us were. That's what makes it real."

The next few hours passed in quiet work. Nia taught Raya how to copy texts without smudging ink. Zee showed her how to recognize metadata fingerprints in damaged files. Mirtha quizzed her gently on quotes and themes.

When it was time to leave, Mirtha stopped her at the door.

"One more thing," she said. "Sooner or later, someone will notice. A teacher. A bot. A parent. Keep your story straight. Don't let them know what you've seen. Not yet."

Raya nodded.

Outside, the sun had set. The stars blinked faintly through the smog. She clutched the journal to her chest, her breath fogging in the cold.

She wasn't just a girl with a library card anymore.

She was part of something larger. Quieter. Dangerous.

She was a memory keeper.

And memories—real ones—could never be deleted.

5
The Last Book

The city was quieter than usual.

Raya noticed it first on the tram the next morning. Fewer people. Fewer voices. Everyone glued to their screens, brows furrowed. The overhead bulletin flashed a new message in bold red: *"Unauthorized Learning Detection Increase. Report Suspicious Activity."*

By the time she arrived at school, three students had already been pulled aside by security drones for "search history anomalies." The atmosphere was tight, like the air had grown heavier.

Jay found her by the hydrogarden wall.

"They're looking for someone," he said.

"You think it's us?"

"I think it's you."

Raya's stomach sank. "But I haven't told anyone."

Jay nodded. "Doesn't matter. They trace curiosity now. Patterns. You asked too many questions."

She thought of the books, the voices, the stories sleeping in ink below the ground.

"What do we do?" she whispered.

"We move the archive. All of it."

Raya stared. "We can't. It's huge."

Jay's voice was firm. "We don't need everything. Just one. One book. The right one."

That night, they returned to Archive Node B. Mirtha was already packing.

"We've been expecting this," she said calmly. "Every safehouse is temporary. Every story, a candle in the wind."

Zee and Nia were sorting crates, salvaging pages, hiding digital traces. But Mirtha handed Raya a different task.

"You must choose the book," she said. "The one we'll carry if everything else burns."

Raya froze. "Me?"

"You found the card. You asked the first question. You read with wonder."

She looked around. Shelves and shelves. So many stories. How could she pick just one?

She ran her fingers along the spines: The Giver, Fahrenheit 451, Anne Frank, The Hobbit, Malala's Story...

They all mattered.

Then she saw it. Thin. Blue. Handwritten title.

The Last Library Card.

Raya pulled it down. It wasn't printed. It was a journal—blank pages at the end, but the beginning was filled with the story of someone like her. Someone who had found a card, followed riddles, joined the Pagekeepers. The voice was younger than Mirtha's, older than hers.

"I found the first story," the final entry read. "But this is not the last. Whoever reads this next—keep going. Add your voice. One book becomes many."

Raya turned to the blank pages. Without hesitation, she opened her pen and began to write.

"My name is Raya Sharma. I live in a world where asking is dangerous, and knowing is worse. But I asked. I followed a lion. I found voices in pages. I became a keeper..."

She wrote until her hand cramped.

When she was done, she closed the journal and handed it to Mirtha.

"This one," she said.

Mirtha pressed the book to her chest like it was a heartbeat.

The next day, they split up. Each Pagekeeper took a path. Jay went east. Zee and Nia disappeared through the old sewer networks. Mirtha stayed behind to wipe the node.

Raya took a route she had never taken before—through abandoned schools, empty lecture halls, and shattered screen towers. She wore the journal in a hidden pouch, close to her skin.

But the city wasn't blind.

Two streets from her safe zone, she heard the buzz.

Drones. Four of them. Black and chrome, unblinking.

She turned and ran. Not for herself. For the story.

She darted down an alley, climbed a trash chute, slid under a gate. Her breath tore from her lungs. Her legs ached. But she didn't stop.

She reached the edge of the Memory Field—an old power station shielded from signals. No drones crossed it. She ducked behind a rusted van just as the hum faded.

Safe.

For now.

She sat in the dirt, catching her breath. Then she pulled the journal from its pouch.

It was still there. Still whole.

She opened the last page and added three words:

"Still running. Still remembering."

That night, she buried the journal in a waterproof box beneath the roots of an old banyan tree. A lion was carved into the trunk.

She didn't know who would find it next. But someone would.

Someone always did.

And when they did, they'd read the truth: about stories, about memory, about quiet resistance.

Because books don't die.

They wait.

And *The Last Library Card* still had pages to fill.

--THE END----------------------------

This story was inspired by the idea that even in a world full of technology, books and stories still matter. I imagined a future where books were forgotten, and one curious reader brought them back. I hope this story makes you think, imagine, and maybe even pick up a book you've never read before.

Thank you for reading The Last Library Card.